"Are you troubled by strange noises in the night?
Do you experience feelings of dread in your basement or attic?
If the answer is yes, then don't wait another minute.
Pick up your phone and call the professionals. . .
GHOSTBUSTERS."
    So that's what Dana did, and the Ghostbusters were
on their way to fame and fortune!
They were coming. . .TO SAVE THE WORLD!

GH STBUSTERS

A Storybook by Anne Digby

SCHOLASTIC INC.
New York Toronto London Auckland Sydney Tokyo

BILL MURRAY   DAN AYKROYD
SIGOURNEY WEAVER

GHOSTBUSTERS

COLUMBIA PICTURES PRESENTS
AN IVAN REITMAN FILM
A BLACK RHINO/BERNIE BRILLSTEIN PRODUCTION
"GHOSTBUSTERS"
ALSO STARRING HAROLD RAMIS   RICK MORANIS

MUSIC BY ELMER BERNSTEIN "GHOSTBUSTERS" PERFORMED BY RAY PARKER, JR. PRODUCTION DESIGN BY JOHN DE CUIR

DIRECTOR OF PHOTOGRAPHY LASZLO KOVACS, A.S.C. VISUAL EFFECTS BY RICHARD EDLUND, A.S.C. EXECUTIVE PRODUCER BERNIE BRILLSTEIN

WRITTEN BY DAN AYKROYD AND HAROLD RAMIS PRODUCED AND DIRECTED BY IVAN REITMAN

ISBN 0-590-33684-3

12 11 10 9 8 7 6 5 4 3 2 1   1   5 6 7 8 9/8 0/9

Printed in the U.S.A.   18

The Storybook of the Film

1

The very first sign that something peculiar was happening to the city of New York was the ghostly manifestation one lunch hour in the public library on Fifth Avenue. You expect to find a few books written by ghost writers in a public library, but this was something entirely different. Alice, one of the librarians, was stacking books back onto the shelves from a library cart and humming to herself when suddenly —

Whoosh!

A pile of books floated off the cart and stacked themselves.

Crr-eakkkkkk!

A drawer slid open and some catalog cards flew out.

Alice stared in horror. Then another drawer slid open, and another. Cards started flying in all directions! Trembling and panic-stricken, the librarian started to run down the long aisle between the bookcases to escape the flying cards. As she reached the end of the first row and turned the corner, a huge gust of wind blew into her face and with a sudden unearthly flash of light, there it was —

The ghost.

Alice screamed and fainted.

It was a paranormal happening of such intensity that when Spengler — who was one of the first on the scene — took a psycho-kinetic energy reading on his meter, the needle went right off the top of the scale. Spengler was so excited that his glasses nearly fell off as he stared at it.

He rushed to find a telephone booth, pushing his way through the goggle-eyed crowd outside the public library, and called up Ray Stantz at the university. "Get over here fast, Ray — bring Venkman. New York Public Library on Fifth Avenue. Something big happened at 1:40 p.m. Ten people witnessed it — a free floating, full torso, vaporous apparition. It blew books off shelves from yards away and scared the socks off some poor librarian. I've taken PKE valences and it's buried the needle!"

"I know for a fact Pete's busy with his research this afternoon."

"Come off it, Ray. Research nothing! This is the big one!"

It was big, sure enough. But it was nothing compared with things to come.

Without the Ghostbusters, New York would have been sunk.

Of course, they weren't the Ghostbusters then. They were just three ordinary, brilliant, young research scientists: serious, dedicated, and scholarly. At least, that's the impression they must have given at some time to the Board of Regents at Weaver Hall University in New York. The Board had awarded them generous funds and laboratory space at the university's Department of Psychology to enable them to conduct research into the paranormal. The Board then sat back to wait for Dr. Peter Venkman, Dr. Ray Stantz, and Dr. Egon Spengler to come up with some spine-tingling results.

They'd been waiting an awfully long time and their patience was now exhausted. Although Peter Venkman, Ray Stantz, and Egon Spengler didn't yet know it, their days at Weaver Hall were numbered.

On the day of the library ghost, Pete Venkman was in his laboratory indulging in an idle experiment. A pretty, young Weaver Hall student named Jennifer was helping him with his research into extrasensory perception. She had to guess what was on the ESP cards and got lots of encouragement from Venkman each time she guessed, even when the answer was wrong. The male student who was taking part in the experiment with them didn't fare so well. He got back a tiny shock

from an electrode attached to his hand each time he guessed, even when the answer was right.

"What are you trying to prove?" he yelled in a fury.

"I'm studying the effect of negative reinforcement on ESP," replied Venkman.

"I'll tell you what the effect is. I'm going! Keep the five bucks!"

"Then my theory is correct!" said Venkman. As the male student stormed out, he put a hand on the girl's arm.

"You better get used to that, Jennifer. It's the kind of resentment that your ability provokes in people."

"Do you think I have it, Dr. Venkman?"

Venkman never got any further because at that moment Ray Stantz burst in with the news of the library ghost.

"Did those ultraviolet lenses come in for the video camera? And that blank tape — where is it? We need it. This is it, Pete. This is definitely it! Come on, Spengler wants us both down at the library."

"Can't you see I'm right in the middle of something, Ray? I need more time with this subject."

"Come on."

Venkman grumbled all the way to the New York Public Library.

"You two guys have finally gone around the bend on this ghost business. You're always running around New York talking to every schizo in town who thinks he's had a paranormal experience. And where does it get you, Ray?"

"You seem to forget, Pete, that I was present at an undersea, unexplained mass sponge migration."

"Oh, sure. The sponges migrated about a yard and a half."

They met up with Spengler outside and the

three of them went in to meet the head librarian. "Thank you for coming. I hope we can clear this up quickly and quietly."

"Let's not rush things," grinned Venkman. "We don't even know what you have yet."

Nearby, Alice was lying stretched out on a table with a medical orderly fussing around her. "I don't remember seeing any legs, but it definitely had arms because it reached out for me," she told them.

"I can't wait to get a look at this thing!" said Stantz, who'd brought the video camera. "I'll get pictures!"

Spengler was already on his way back down to the basement with the lights on his PKE meter flashing. "I'm going to get some more readings!"

Venkman just looked down at the prone librarian. "Alice, I'm going to ask you a couple of standard questions, okay? Have you ever been diagnosed schizophrenic, mentally incompetent? Are you a habitual user of drugs, stimulants, alcohol?"

She could only look at him, dazed.

Then suddenly Spengler was back, waving his meter. "It's down there! It's moving! Quick!"

The three of them raced down to the basement. "Look!" yelled Spengler. In one of the aisles between the rows of bookshelves, a stack of books was piled from floor to ceiling. He bent towards it and took a PKE reading. "This is hot! Full of paranormal activity!"

Ray Stantz advanced on the stack, taping with the videocamera, as he walked. "Symmetrical book stacking. Just like the Philadelphia mass turbulence of 1947."

"You're right," said Peter Venkman, rolling his eyes. "No human being would stack books like this."

A moment later they saw the drawers that had held the catalog cards. They were open and thick green goo was dripping out of them. "Talk about telekinetic activity. Look at this mess!" said Stantz. "Ectoplasmic residue. Ghost goo! The real thing!"

"Get a sample, Venkman," said Spengler. "I'd like to analyze it."

He was taking meter readings again now, advancing up the next aisle. "Come on, I'm getting stronger readings." Meanwhile Venkman was struggling to get some of the goo in a container; it was sticking to his hands and bouncing around when he tried to shake it off. "Uggh!"

"*It's here!*" squeaked Spengler, as the three of them rounded the next corner.

They stared, openmouthed. The library ghost! The phantom of an elderly woman stood in the aisle. She was running her finger along the bookshelf, looking for a book. She found it, took it out, and started to read.

"A full torso apparition, and it's real," whispered Stantz. The three of them ducked behind a bookcase, knees knocking. "What do we do now?" It was decided that Venkman should try to make contact.

He advanced slowly on the ghost. Behind him Stantz peered out with the camera, videotaping feverishly.

"Hello," said Venkman to the ghost. "I'm Peter."

It ignored him.

"Er — where are you from? Originally, that is."

The library ghost turned and put a finger to her lips to quiet him. "Sssssssh."

Venkman gazed at the other two helplessly. It wasn't working.

"We'll grab her then!" whispered Stantz. "Get ready. . . ."

The three of them crept up on the ghost and reached out their hands to take hold of her. . . .

Ahhhhhhhhhhh!

They screamed as the peaceful, elderly library ghost exploded into a vicious white-haired skeleton, rising up over them.

They ran. As fast as their legs could carry them. Up the stairs, through the main library and out onto Fifth Avenue.

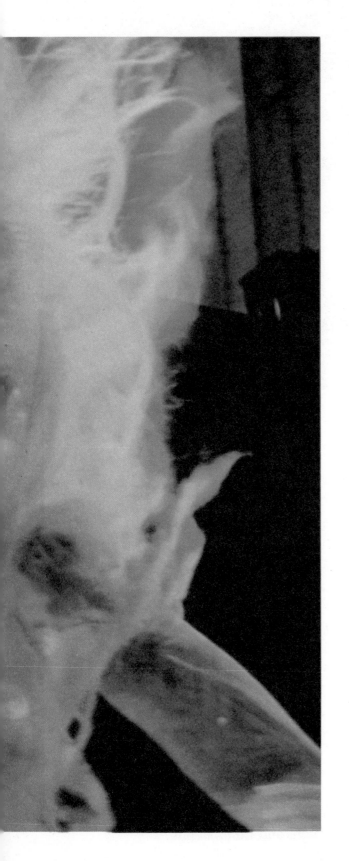

"Did you see it? What was it?" the head librarian called out to the fleeing figures.

"We'll get back to you!" Stantz yelled. And they were gone.

They were shaking with triumph by the time they got back to the university. "I . . . I just got overexcited, but wasn't it incredible, Pete?" gasped Stantz. "I mean, we actually touched the etheric plane. You know what this could mean to the university."

"It'll be bigger than the micro chip," pronounced Venkman.

"We have an excellent chance of actually catching a ghost and holding it," said Spengler, adjusting his glasses and checking over his meter readings as they walked along. "Wait till the Dean hears about this!"

In fact the Dean was waiting for them in their quarters, and some removal men were shifting pieces of equipment out of their laboratory.

"Hey, Dean Yeager!" exclaimed Pete Venkman, exuberantly. "I trust you're moving us to better quarters on campus."

"No," said the Dean. "You're being moved *off* campus. The Board of Regents has decided to terminate your grant. You are to vacate these premises immediately."

"I demand an explanation!" said Venkman.

"Fine. This university will no longer fund any of your activities. Your theories are the worst kind of popular tripe. Your methods are sloppy and questionable. You are a poor scientist."

"I see," said Venkman, looking very downcast.

"You have no place in this university," ended the Dean.

So that was that. Doctors Venkman, Stantz, and Spengler were out on their ears. Their careers as research scientists were over. For the first time in their lives they were going to have to earn an honest living out in the harsh, commercial world.

It was fate.

"I believe everything happens for a reason," said Venkman when they were alone. "We were destined to be thrown out of this dump. To go into business for ourselves. We're on the threshold of establishing the indispensable defense science of the next decade. Professional Paranormal Investigations and Eliminations."

"Ecto-containment!" said Spengler.

"Ghostbusting!" echoed Stantz, in delight.

"The franchise rights alone will make us rich beyond our dreams," Venkman added. "Come on, let's find some premises. . . ."

"Uniforms! We'll need jumpsuits and nuclear proton backpacks, laser stream throwers — you name it, we need it."

"We also have to design the infallible ecto-container, by which I mean ghost trap. . . ." said Stantz.

"And buy ourselves an Ectomobile — sirens, flashing lights, the whole works. Flying squad to eliminate paranormal presences at any time of the day or night. Oh, Pete," said Spengler, "let's shake on it."

They laughed. You couldn't keep these three down for long.

The Ghostbusters were about to hit New York.

And not a moment too soon.

2

One of the first things the Ghostbusters did, after setting up shop in a vacant fire station in downtown New York (mainly because Stantz fell in love with the idea of sliding down the pole every time they were called out), was to get a one-shot TV commercial made. They could only afford the one shot.

"We'll never get any business if nobody knows about us," said Venkman.

Luckily, a certain Ms. Dana Barrett happened to see that TV commercial when she got home from work one day, or things might have turned out even worse for her. (And that's really saying something.)

Dana was a very beautiful young woman, a professional cellist, and she lived in a penthouse on the twenty-second floor of the Shandor apartments on Central Park West. The Shandor was an old-fashioned skyscraper, designed and built not long after the

First World War by an obscure architect called Ivo Shandor.

Dana staggered into her apartment, carrying her cello case and a bag full of groceries. As she turned on the TV, she only half noticed Venkman, Spengler, and Stantz jumping about on the screen. They were dressed in uniform, identical gray jumpsuits, each wearing a backpack, and they were shooting laser streams up into the sky from fancy pieces of equipment.

Are you troubled by strange noises in the night?

Do you experience feelings of dread in your basement or attic?

Dana just smiled to herself. She was thinking that she'd better go to Louis' party next week. Louis Tully was her lovelorn next-door neighbor: a middle-aged self-employed tax accountant. He was always trying to be friendly. He'd met her just now as she'd stepped out of the elevator, and asked her to the party for the tenth time. "Listen, I'm having a big party for all my clients. My fourth anniversary as an accountant. And even though you do your own tax return, I'd like you to stop by." She'd told him she'd try to.

Have you ever seen a spook, specter, or ghost?

Dana frowned at the TV. What *were* they talking about?

If the answer is yes, then don't wait another minute. Pick up your phone and call the professionals . . .

GHOSTBUSTERS!

Our courteous and efficient staff is on call twenty-four hours a day to serve your supernatural elimination needs.

The three figures pointed at her.

We're ready to believe you.

Dana just stared in amazement and then walked across and turned off the TV set. "Ghostbusters!" she giggled.

She went into the kitchen and started unpacking her groceries.

She put a large carton of eggs on the kitchen counter.

The lid flew open of its own accord. Dana

stared. The eggs were bouncing and shaking in the carton. Then the shells exploded open and egg yolks flew out.

Two eggs started cooking and sizzling on top of the counter.

Two more flew past her.

She wanted to scream. Then — sud-

denly — she knew she had to go and look in the refrigerator. There seemed to be yellow flames belching out of it. She walked over and opened the door.

This time she really did scream.

There was a blinding yellow light everywhere — the flames of a fiery volcano raged inside the refrigerator — and down there in the flames was a temple, and writhing, snarling animals. A stone dog snarled up at her, as though about to pounce. A terror dog!

"Eeeeeeeeeek!" screamed Dana.

A cold, sinister voice from inside the refrigerator cried:

"Zuul."

Dana slammed the refrigerator door shut and raced out of the kitchen. "Oh!" she sobbed.

The Ghostbusters had their first customer.

 ★★★ ★★★

Dana turned up at the old fire station two days later. Up 'til then, the Ghostbusters had been feeling very low. They'd put up a huge banner outside but no one seemed to have noticed it. They hadn't had a single telephone call so far. Janine, the secretary they'd hired, had nothing to do. Today Stantz had spent $5000 on a broken-down old Cadillac ambulance complete with sirens and flashing lights. The Ectomobile. Of course, they had to have an Ectomobile — to carry their ecto-containers (they'd made some really good ones that they hoped would trap the nastiest ghosts) and the rest of their ghost-busting equipment. But it had cleaned them out.

So when Dana walked in and told her story, it was a big thrill.

". . . and this voice said 'Zuul' . . . and I slammed the refrigerator door and I left. That was two days ago, and I — I haven't been back to my apartment."

"Generally, you don't see that kind of behavior in a major appliance," said Venkman. "What do you think it was?"

"If I knew what it was, I wouldn't be here," said Dana. She was sitting in a chair with two electrodes attached to the side of her head while Spengler monitored her on the computer screen.

"She's telling the truth, Venkman. At least, she thinks she is."

"Good!" said Venkman, with pleasure. He liked the look of Dana Barrett. He'd like to get to know her better. "Well, Miss Barrett, there are things we can do, standard procedures in a case like this, which often bring results."

"I can go to the Hall of Records," said Stantz eagerly, "and check out the structural details of the building. And maybe the building itself has a history of psychic turbulence."

"Good idea, Ray," said Venkman.

"And I can look for the name 'Zuul' in the usual literature," said Spengler. "*Spates Catalog. Tobin's Spirit Guide.*"

"Great," said Venkman. "And I'll take Miss Barrett back to her apartment and check her out — I mean, check the apartment out. Okay?"

But when Peter Venkman took Dana back to her apartment on the twenty-second floor of the Shandor building he drew a blank in every direction. The only thing he could find in the refrigerator was junk food. And when he ran the detector rod all over the apartment the PKE meter registered zero. Worst of all, when he said: "Dana, I am madly in love with you," the atmosphere became very chilly.

"Will you please leave?" she said.

As she pushed him out into the hall, Peter said:

"I'll prove myself to you! I'll solve your problem. And then you'll say Pete Venkman's a guy who can get things done. Okay? I bet you're gonna be thinking about me after I'm gone."

"I bet I am," said Dana.

Louis appeared in the hall from his next-door apartment. "You all right, Dana?" But she'd already slammed the door.

Venkman took the elevator and left.

"I'm going to need some petty cash," he told the other two when he got back to the fire station. He found them eating a cheap Chinese take-out meal in the upstairs kitchen. "I should take Dana out to dinner. Our first and only customer. We don't want to lose her."

"We haven't got any petty cash," said Stantz. "We're broke."

Downstairs in the office, the phone rang and Janine took the call. "Hello, Ghostbusters. . . . You do?. . . . You have? No kidding? Yes, of course they'll be totally discreet."

She jumped up in the air with joy. "We got one! An assignment!"

Upstairs the red light flashed for the first time and the alarm bell rang. The three Ghostbusters looked at each other in disbelief.

"It's a call!" exclaimed Stantz. "Wheeee!"

Before you could say "ectoplasm" the three Ghostbusters had slid down the fireman's pole, grabbed their uniforms and nuclear proton backpacks from their downstairs lockers, and leapt aboard the Ectomobile.

"Where's the job, Janine?" yelled Venkman.

"The Sedgewick Hotel, Dr. Venkman. There's big trouble. A ghost on the twelfth floor."

"Sedgewick Hotel — here we come."

"The manager doesn't want the guests upset. He wants you to be discreet."

"Sure!"

With sirens screaming and headlights blazing the Ectomobile sped out into the night, its flashing lights turning atop its roof, its brakes squealing as it rounded each corner and headed for the center of the city.

The Ghostbusters were on their way.

3

It wasn't easy trapping the ghost at the Sedgewick Hotel — but they did it in the end. It was a nasty little green spook that flitted around slurping up everybody's food.

"Are you guys astronauts?" asked one of the hotel guests, as they raced in to take the elevator to the twelfth floor, laser stream guns at the ready.

"No, exterminators," said Venkman. "Someone saw a cockroach on twelve."

"That's got to be some cockroach!"

Up on twelve they tested their laser guns at long range on a cart loaded with toilet paper rolls, and they worked beautifully. The rolls all sizzled up. "We must never, ever let our laser streams cross," warned Spengler. "That would be very dangerous." Then they split up around the corridors to find the ghost, keeping in touch by means of their walkie-talkie radios. Venkman was the first to get entangled with it, and it covered him in green goo.

"He slimed me!" he wailed over the walkie-talkie.

"Great!" replied Stantz. "Actual physical contact!"

Then Egon came in: "Save some for me, Pete."

Several smashed chandeliers and overturned banquet tables later, they finally brought the ghost down with the laser streams in the State Ballroom of the Sedgewick Hotel and entrapped it in the ecto-container. They walked out with the smoking ghost trap into the big foyer, where the manager had been holding back scores of guests. The guests had been waiting to go into their banquet and couldn't understand what all the noise had been about in there.

"Didn't you see it? What is it?" asked the anxious manager.

"We got it," said Stantz, holding up the steaming ghost trap in triumph for everybody to see. The smell was terrible. "A class-five full vapor. A real nasty one, too!"

"It's going to be really something keeping the beast stored and making sure we recharge the trap, but luckily we're doing a special offer on proton charging and storage this week," said Venkman. He made some quick jottings. "So the bill comes to just five thousand dollars."

"Five thousand dollars? I had no idea it

would be so much. I won't pay it."

"We can just put it right back in the ball-room then," said Venkman, about to crumple up the bill.

"No!" cried the manager, snatching the bill. "I'll pay. *Anything!*"

"Thanks so much," said Venkman.

The Ghostbusters were in business.

Their triumph at the Sedgewick Hotel brought the Ghostbusters overnight fame. They were featured in the newspapers, on radio, on television. And now everybody wanted them.

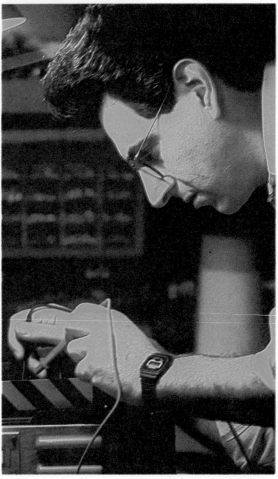

There was something rotten in the state of New York. The city was suddenly abnormally charged with psychokinetic energy and there were ghost sightings everywhere.

The Ectomobile became a familiar sight at night around the city streets, siren screaming, lights flashing, as the Ghostbusters raced here, there and everywhere, rounding up obnoxious ghosts and bringing them back to their HQ in steaming, stinking ghost traps.

In the basement of the old fire station Spengler had designed a foolproof storage facility for the laser-stunned ghosts in their smoking containers. The storage area was protected by a high voltage grid, to make sure none of the ghosts could ever escape.

It was foolproof; that is, unless somebody stupid switched off the protection grid.

The Ghostbusters were kept so busy that they told Janine to hire a fourth man. She found them somebody called Winston Zeddemore.

"Welcome aboard," said Venkman, when he and Stantz returned from a particularly exhausting all-night stint at a fashionable dance club, and found Winston at their HQ. "Here, hold this." They handed him a smoking ghost trap, and he took it, holding his nose.

Meanwhile over in her penthouse on Central Park West, Dana Barrett was listening to the early morning news bulletin on the radio:

"The boys slugged it out with a bothersome ghost at a fashionable dance club, The Rose, and stayed to dance the night away with some of the lovely ladies there."

Dana sighed. She'd misjudged Peter Venkman. He seemed to know about ghostbusting all right. He seemed to be getting pretty famous.

So when she came out of the Metropolitan Opera House after a rehearsal that day, and spotted Venkman standing by the fountain across the plaza, she hurried over to speak to him.

"You're a big celebrity now. Do you have any information on my case?"

"I prefer to tell you in private."

"Tell me now."

"Well, okay," said Venkman. "I found the name Zuul for you." He pulled a piece of paper from his pocket and consulted it. "The name Zuul refers to a demi-god worshipped around 6,000 B.C. by the Sumerians."

Dana took the piece of paper from him excitedly and read it.

" 'Zuul was the minion of Gozer.' What's Gozer?"

"Gozer was very big in Sumeria," Venkman explained. "Big guy."

"Well, what's he doing in my refrigerator?" asked Dana.

"I'm working on that. If we could get together tonight, around 9 o'clock, we could exchange information."

"Oh, okay. I'll . . . uh . . . see you tonight."

"I'll bring *The Roylance Guide* and we'll eat and read," he grinned. Venkman went off across the plaza past a twirling roller skater and gave a happy little twirl himself.

★★★   ★★★

When Venkman got back to HQ, Janine told him there was a man waiting to see him in his office.

"He's a government official. From the Environmental Protection Agency. Something about pollution. He looks grim."

Venkman marched in.

"Can I help you?"

"I'm Walter Peck. I represent the Environmental Protection Agency, third district. Are you Peter Venkman?"

"Yes, I'm . . . Dr. Venkman."

"Exactly what are you a doctor of, Mr. Venkman?"

"Well, I have PhDs in parapsychology and psychology."

"I see. And now you catch ghosts. Where do you put them?"

"In a storage facility in the basement."

"May I see it?"

"No."

"There have been stories in the media, Mr. Venkman, and we want to assess any possible environmental impact from your operation. For instance, the presence of noxious, possibly hazardous waste chemicals in your basement. Either you show me what is down there or I'll get a court order."

"You go and get a court order, then," said Venkman.

Walter Peck rose to his feet. "Very well, Mr. Venkman. Have it your own way."

He picked up his briefcase and left.

Venkman went straight down to the basement after that. The other three were all down there. Stantz had been instructing Winston in the technology of the ecto-storage system. It was very complicated, storing all those noxious vapors, entities, and slimes and keeping them inert in their loaded traps.

"How's the protection grid?" asked Venkman uneasily. "We just had a visit from the EPA." He looked across at Spengler, who was frowning through his glasses and reading some figures on a clipboard. "What's the matter with you, Egon?"

"I'm worried," said Spengler. "The grid's not too good. It's getting crowded in there. All these readings I've taken, they point to something big coming."

"What do you mean, big?" asked Winston.

Spengler held up a Twinkie.

"Let's say this represents the normal amount of psychokinetic energy in New York. Well, today's readings would represent a Twinkie 35 feet long, weighing 600 pounds."

"That's a big Twinkie," said Winston.

Spengler gave a sage nod, and then ate it.

"We could be on the verge of a fourfold crossrip — a PKE surge of incredible, even dangerous proportions!"

Soon after dark that night a fork of lightning struck the flat roof of the Shandor apartments high up against the Manhattan skyline. And in the livid light the roof was transformed into a temple.

Outside the gates of that temple, two stone statues stood guard — the statues of terror dogs.

Then, as the thunder rolled and smoke scudded across the rooftop, the stone casing of the statues began to crumble away, revealing the glowing red eyes and the moving claws of the live monster dogs inside.

4

Dana Barrett noticed the lightning as she stepped out of the elevator on the twenty-second floor, nibbling popcorn, but she was more concerned about giving Louis Tully the slip. He'd been listening for her and now he appeared. "It's my party tonight, Dana!" said the plump little accountant. "Don't say you've forgotten."

"Oh, Louis, I've got a date tonight. He's coming at 9 o'clock."

An hour later, relaxing in an armchair in her apartment and thinking about what she was going to wear for her date with Peter Venkman, Dana suddenly screeched.

Long, scaly arms appeared out of the armchair. A huge clawed hand clapped itself over her mouth to muffle her cries as it dragged her, struggling and sobbing, into the kitchen.

★★★　　　★★★

In Louis' apartment next door, the party was in full swing. As some late arrivals went through to the bedroom to throw their coats on the bed, Louis noticed something peculiar lying there, under some coats. Growling.

"So who brought the dog?" he asked.

Then they all screamed as the huge beast launched itself out of the bedroom and rampaged through the party, scattering guests in all directions.

It was making straight for Louis.

With a yell of terror he raced out of his apartment, with the monster in hot pursuit, sped down in the elevator and burst out into

the street. "Help! Help! There's a bear after me!"

The creature pursued him right across Central Park. Puffing and panting, Louis saw the lighted windows of the Tavern-on-the-Green restaurant. He raced up and hammered on the window, the monster close behind him. "Help me!" But the people inside were enjoying themselves and just continued eating.

Suddenly a huge claw grabbed hold of Louis and dragged him away into the night, screaming. . . .

High up on the roof of the Shandor building, where the two terror dog statues had been, there were now just two empty pedestals.

They had selected their victims and had now possessed them.

★★★   ★★★

When Pete Venkman stepped out of his taxi at 9 o'clock, holding a bunch of roses for Dana, he saw police all around the building. "What happened?" he asked the doorman.

"Some moron brought a cougar to a party up on twenty-two and it went berserk."

Peter noticed more police when he got up there, questioning the party guests. He went straight over to Dana's door and knocked.

As soon as she opened the door to him, he knew there was something different about her. She was wearing an amazing orange dress and lots of exotic makeup.

"That's a different look for you, isn't it?" he said in surprise.

"Are you the Keymaster?" she replied.

"Er, not that I know of," said Peter, a shiver running down his spine.

Dana shut the door in his face. Recovering quickly, he banged hard again.

"I'm a friend of his! He told me to meet him here!"

This time she let him into the apartment.

"I didn't get your name," said Venkman.

"I am Zuul," replied Dana. "I am the Gatekeeper."

"What are we doing today?" he asked nervously.

"We must prepare for the coming of Gozer, the Destructor," she said, putting her arms around him.

"I guess the roses worked, huh?" said Venkman as she hugged him savagely. "Hey, take it easy."

He got free of her, sweat breaking out on his brow. "I make it a rule never to get involved with possessed people," he told her. "I mean, you know the old saying. 'Two's company, three's a crowd.' "

He pushed her away again. "Relax," he said. "That's better. What I'd really like to do is talk to Dana . . . *Dana*? It's Peter."

"There is no Dana," came the cold, distant reply. "There is only Zuul."

"Zuul, you nut. . . ."

She growled at him demonically, eyes rolling, head thrashing back and forth.

"No Dana, only Zuul!"

She floated up into the air, high above his head, then turned over and looked down at him.

"Please come down," he begged.

But she just roared in his face.

Meanwhile, Louis Tully was scaring the life out of people in Central Park. Wild and red-eyed, he was running up to them:

"I am the Keymaster! The Destructor will come! I must find the destroyer. I am Vinz Clortho, Keymaster of Gozer. Are you the Gatekeeper?"

The police rounded him up, put him in a strait jacket, and delivered him by van to the Ghostbusters' HQ. They carried him in and handed him over to Egon Spengler, who was alone there on night duty with Janine. Ray

and Winston were out in the Ectomobile.

"You a ghostbuster?" said the sergeant. "We got this guy. Bellevue doesn't want him."

Spengler ran the ghost sensor over him and nodded. "We'll take him."

"Are you the Gatekeeper?" asked Louis. "I'm looking for the Gatekeeper."

Spengler sat him in a chair and wired him up to the computer monitor. A terror dog's head appeared on the screen. Spengler was filled with unease. "What did you say your name was?"

"Vinz Clortho, Keymaster of Gozer."

"Well, according to this, his name's Louis Tully," said Janine, checking through his wallet. "He lives on Central Park West."

She looked at Spengler, feeling scared as Louis picked up a piece of pizza and wiped it down his cheek.

"There's something very strange about that man. I have a terrible feeling that something awful's going to happen."

At that moment, the phone rang.

"Egon, it's Peter. I have some news from the world of Gozer. I'm here with Dana Barrett. I've had to put her out cold with a shot of tranquilizers. She says she's the Gatekeeper. Does that make any sense?"

"Some," replied Spengler. "I've just met the Keymaster. He's here with me."

"Maybe we should get them together."

"I think that would be extraordinarily dangerous," said Spengler.

"Okay, well hold on to him," said Venkman. "I'll be with you soon."

Tenderly he looked down at the unconscious figure of Dana, kissed her on the hand and then left.

★★★   ★★★

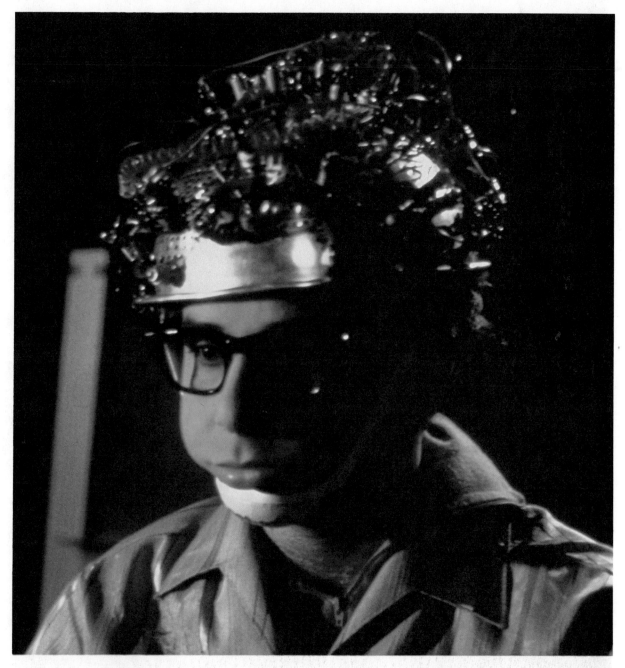

Ray Stantz and Winston Zeddemore were on patrol duty, cruising the city streets in the Ectomobile. Winston was driving and Ray was examining some blueprints on his lap.

"What are you so involved with there?" asked Winston.

"These are the blueprints for the structural ironwork in Dana Barrett's building, and they're very, very strange."

"Hey, Ray, do you remember something in the Old Testament about the last day, when the dead would rise from the grave?"

"Judgment Day?" said Stantz. "Yeah. Every religion has its own myth about the end of the world."

"Myth?" Winston gave a hollow laugh. "Ray, has it ever occurred to you that maybe the reason we've been so busy lately is because the dead have been rising from the grave?"

Stantz shivered.

He would have shivered some more if he'd realized just how close the crisis was. It came in the shape of Walter Peck, the government official from the Environmental Protection Agency.

And for the city of New York, it was very nearly the end of the world.

5

Walter Peck barged his way into the old fire station the next morning, flanked by a police officer and an electric company official. He waved a warrant in Janine's face. "Step aside, miss, or I'll have you arrested for interfering with a police officer."

"What's that you're holding?"

"It's a cease and desist all commerce order, seizure of premises and chattels, ban on the use of public utilities for unlicensed waste-handlers, and a federal entry and inspection order."

Egon Spengler was down in the basement area with Louis at the time, conducting one last test. He was taken by surprise when they came marching down there. "Egon! I tried to stop them!" cried Janine. "He says they have a warrant."

Peck just pointed to the electrical boxes on the wall that powered the protection grid and rapped an order to the electric company official:

"Shut all these off."

"Don't!" cried Spengler. "It would be extremely hazardous — "

"I'll tell you what's hazardous," said Peck. "You're facing federal prosecution for at least six environmental violations. We're going to shut off those beams."

"Try to understand," said Spengler. "This is a high-voltage laser containment system — turning it off would be like dropping a bomb on the city."

"He's right!" said Venkman, coming slowly down the steps.

"Don't patronize me!" said Peck. "I'm not grotesquely stupid like the people you dupe."

"He wants to shut down the grid, Pete," said Spengler helplessly.

"If you shut that down, we won't be responsible for what happens. . . . " began Venkman.

"Shut it off!" Peck ordered again.

The electric company man raised his hand toward the switch while Louis watched excitedly. Venkman and Spengler rushed forward to try and stop him. . . .

Too late.

He pushed down the switch. All the lights dimmed.

Red lights started flashing everywhere and alarm bells began ringing. Bright lights started to shine all around the ghost containment boxes as they began to break open.

"Clear the building!" screamed Spengler. "Run for it!"

They all raced upstairs and out into the street, just as the fire station began to explode behind them. Explosion after explosion!

A huge crowd gathered, openmouthed, standing well back and watching the smoke and sparks flying and the building falling apart. And then a huge ball of fire shot out through its roof and a column of flame rose into the sky.

There was dust in the air, the crash of falling debris, the wail of police sirens.

But Louis Tully just stared at that column of flame, transfixed.

"This is what I've been waiting for from Gozer!" he whispered. "This is it. This is the sign!"

"Yeah, it's a sign all right," said Janine. "It says we're going out of business."

But Louis had already fled.

By the time Ray and Winston showed up in the Ectomobile, the police had erected barriers to hold the crowds back. "What happened?" asked Ray.

"The storage facility blew," said Spengler. "They shut off the protection grid."

Venkman came running up, looking alarmed.

"Where's the Keymaster?"

He and Spengler looked at each other in horror. Louis had escaped. They had to catch him!

"Come on!" Spengler yelled. The four of them went racing off down the street. But at the end of the street, Peck was waiting for them, with a posse of police officers.

"Arrest these men!" he said. "They're in criminal violation of the Environmental Protection Act. And this explosion is a direct result of it."

"You moron!" said Spengler, lunging at Peck.

The four Ghostbusters tried to slug it out with the police but they were overpowered and taken to the city lock-up. And as the police van took them away, the huge column of flame emanating from the fire station suddenly — like a dying rocket — split up into numerous offshoots of ghostly light which then winged their way down to all corners of the city.

The ghosts were free again.

There was terror on the streets of New York. There were ghosts everywhere. They were driving taxicabs and causing pileups. They were winging up from subways. The little green ghost from the Sedgewick Hotel was slurping up the hot dogs from all the hot dog stands in town.

Louis Tully stood in the center of Times Square and stared upward.

He was the Keymaster. He would find the Gatekeeper very soon now. They would worship Gozer together—Gozer, the Destructor.

Up in her penthouse, Dana Barrett stood at the window of her living room, gazing at the ghostly beams in the sky, as though in a trance.

Then the window exploded outward. There was dust and smoke everywhere. She stood there, in the ruins, waiting for the smoke to clear. Waiting for the Keymaster.

★★★   ★★★

Languishing in jail, with plenty of time to think, the Ghostbusters had fitted the last piece of the jigsaw puzzle in place. Stantz was showing them the blueprints of Dana's building.

"The structure of this rooftop is cold-riveted girders with cores of pure selenium. The whole building is a huge superconductive antenna, designed and built expressly for the purpose of pulling in and concentrating spiritual turbulence. So your girlfriend, Pete, lives in the corner penthouse of Spook Central."

"Something terrible is about to enter our world," nodded Spengler, "and this building is obviously the door. The architect's name was Ivo Shandor. I checked him out in *Tobin's Spirit Guide*. After the First World War, Shandor decided that society was too sick to survive. He designed this building and formed a secret society of Gozer worshippers. They conducted bizarre rituals on the roof, intended to bring about the end of the world. And now it looks like it may actually happen."

"And we're locked up in a jail!" moaned Venkman.

But at that very moment a police official arrived and unlocked the door of their cell.

"Okay, Ghostbusters! The mayor wants to see you. The whole of Manhattan Island's going crazy and you're his only hope."

★★★   ★★★

Louis walked into Dana's smoking, dust-filled apartment.

"I am the Keymaster," he said.

She turned and walked toward him.

"And I am the Gatekeeper," she said.

Where Dana's front door had once been there was now a shroud of mist. Gradually it cleared, to reveal a secret staircase. Louis and Dana turned and walked toward it.

Slowly, side by side, they mounted the stairs that would take them up to the temple on the rooftop. And into the presence of Gozer.

6

It was nighttime. The population of New York had taken to the streets. The smoking building with the fiery temple on top could be seen for miles around. Behind the temple the black storm clouds gathered and the lightning seemed to set the sky on fire.

There was a doomsday atmosphere. People were praying in the streets.

Only the Ghostbusters could save New York now.

The Ectomobile rolled toward Central Park West, escorted by police, and the crowds parted to let it through. "Ghostbusters!" the people cheered. "Ghostbusters!"

When the four men descended from the vehicle, and advanced to within fifty yards of the smoking skyscraper, the cheers became feverish. The boys looked very purposeful, dressed in their gray jumpsuits, their gear on their backs.

The cheers changed to cries of terror as the street began to bulge and a huge, steaming crack opened up beneath the Ghostbusters' feet. It swallowed them up. But they managed to scramble their way up the side and crawl out again, and the cheering resumed.

They entered the Shandor building and struggled up all twenty-two flights of stairs to the top, groaning under the weight of their nuclear backpacks and lasers. But they made it. Venkman took them through Dana's wrecked apartment, then straight up the secret staircase to the roof. "Look!" whispered Stantz.

Dana and Louis stood on opposite pedestals, arms outflung toward the temple, from which a mysterious glowing light emanated.

"Dana!" cried Venkman. But even as he spoke her name, the two figures became shot through with lightning and turned into the fearful terror dogs, snarling and growling at them ferociously. Then they padded across and sat at the very doors of the temple, as the light from within grew brighter.

The temple doors opened and out of a star-shaped light stepped a sinister-looking woman. She stepped forward and petted each of the terror dogs in turn.

"It's Gozer!" said Ray, gasping. "A woman. Get her!"

But before they could make a move she raised her hands toward them and shot lightning at them from her fingertips. "Die!" she said. The charges of lightning drove the men back, to the very edge of the roof. They dangled over the side of the building, hanging on grimly, while the crowd below screamed.

Somehow they managed to pull themselves back onto the roof and started crawling forward toward Gozer, laser guns at the ready. "Heat 'em up," whispered Spengler, and they turned on the nuclear accelerators on their backpacks. "Right! FIRE!"

They blasted Gozer with laser streams, chasing her all around the temple. "I think we've neutronized it," said Stantz, at last.

"No!" said Egon, checking his PKE meter. "Still alive."

An earth tremor ran through Central Park West, upending vehicles and bringing down pieces of plaster and stone from the buildings.

Then from somewhere inside the temple came the eerie voice of Gozer again.

"Subcreatures! You may choose and perish. You may choose the form of the Destructor."

"Oh, I get it!" said Venkman. "Whoever we think of, whoever comes into our heads — they'll appear and destroy us. So listen, you three," he said urgently, "empty your heads. *Empty your heads*. Don't think of anything."

"The choice is made," cried Gozer. "The Traveler has come."

"Nobody chose anything!" shouted Venkman indignantly.

But Ray Stantz was looking very ashamed of himself.

"I couldn't help it, Pete. It just popped into my head."

"*What* did?"

"I tried to think of the most harmless thing I could. Something I loved from my childhood. Something that could never, ever possibly destroy us."

"Like what?"

"Mr. Stay-Puft, the Marshmallow Man."

From the streets far below there came cries of terror. "You fool, Ray!" said Venkman. "Look down there!"

They crawled to the edge of the roof. A snow-white marshmallow man 150 feet tall was advancing toward the building, roaring and bent on destruction. He was kicking over cars, and people scattered across Central Park in terror.

"I–I used to love Mr. Stay-Puft," said Ray, miserably. "We used to roast marshmallows at camp."

The four Ghostbusters drew their lasers. "Well, let's roast him now!"

They fired down, setting his chest on fire, and he roared with pain. But he was still advancing. The lasers were not strong enough to stop him. He rose into the air — up — up — until he appeared over the edge of the building. He was going to kill them.

"There's only one hope," said Spengler. "Doors to the spirit world swing both ways. We could try to reverse the particle flow through the temple door."

"How?" asked Stantz.

"We have to cross the streams."

"Let our laser streams cross?" exclaimed Venkman. "Excuse me, Egon, you always told us that was very bad. You're going to endanger us. And our client. The nice lady who paid us in advance before she became a dog."

"Not necessarily. There's definitely a very slim chance we'll survive," said Spengler.

The flaming marshmallow man came lunging over the side of the building and was almost upon them.

"I love this plan. I'm excited to be a part of it," said Venkman.

"Let's do it," agreed Winston.

"Let's turn them on, Spengler," said Stantz.

The four men raised their laser guns, aimed them in unison at the temple doors, then fired!

The laser streams crossed.

BOOOMMMMMMMMM!
The explosion that followed blew the whole building to pieces, all twenty-two floors. It also blew up the skyscraper next door.

Globules of molten marshmallow showered all over New York. Walter Peck got smothered in it.

But the Ghostbusters were safe. As the storm clouds rolled away and dawn broke, they crawled out of the ruins, covered in marshmallow like everybody else.

They had destroyed Mr. Stay-Puft and in doing so they had destroyed Gozer. They had saved New York!

And Dana was safe, too, lying in the rubble, encased in the statue of the terror dog. Venkman smashed it open and pulled her free, then took her in his arms and gently kissed her.

From the other statue, lying nearby, a voice said:

"What about me?"

They pulled the dog's head off and there was Louis Tully.

"Who *are* you guys?" asked the little accountant.

"Who *are* we? We're the Ghostbusters."

The crowd pressed in all around them, clapping and cheering: "Ghostbusters!" and Louis beamed.

"Who does your taxes?"

At last the police managed to clear the crowds sufficiently to let the boys board the Ectomobile and get away. They watched as it trundled slowly through the city streets into the rosy dawn.

END